The Secret Life of FIGGY MUSTARDO

By **Marsha Wilson Chall**   Illustrated by **Alison Friend**

 KATHERINE TEGEN BOOKS
An Imprint of HarperCollins Publishers

Katherine Tegen Books is an imprint of HarperCollins Publishers.
The Secret Life of Figgy Mustardo
Text copyright © 2016 by Marsha Wilson Chall
Illustrations copyright © 2016 by Alison Friend
All rights reserved. Manufactured in China.
www.harpercollinschildrens.com

ISBN 978-0-06-228582-9

The artist used pencil drawings with digital color
to create the illustrations for this book.
Typography by Rachel Zegar
16 17 18 19 20   SCP   10 9 8 7 6 5 4 3 2 1
❖
First Edition

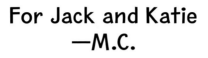

For Jack and Katie
—M.C.

For Lou
—A.F.

More than anything, Figgy loved to play with George Mustardo.

"Figgy, fetch!"

Figgy chased and fetched. And fetched and chased. But sometimes George had other things to do.

Like go to school. "'Bye, Figgy. I'll be back soon," said George.

Figgy waited.

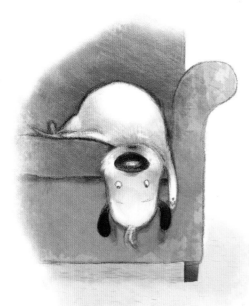

Figgy watched.

Figgy checked the clock.
It said WAY PAST SOON.

But then Figgy found something that looked delicious—George's homework: the history of rock 'n' roll.

He gobbled it up . . .

and fell asleep. Deeper and deeper he slept, and in his dreams, Figgy wasn't just a sleepin', eatin', nothin'-to-do dog anymore.

He was the one, the only
FIGGY "THE HOUND DOG" MUSTARDO!

Who's rockin' the nation?
Who's rollin' the hits?
Who's the hottest dog in town?
Must be "You ain't nothin'
but a hound dog"
FIGGY!

Figgy woke up. *WOOF!* He knew his dream
must be a sign. So he made his own:
FREE ROCK CONCERT!

Everyone rocked! Everyone rolled!
Everyone roared for Figgy to rock! Rock! Rock!
He rocked until he couldn't roll anymore.

"Figgy, we're home! Wanna fetch? Wanna chase?"

Figgy just curled 'round his tail and snoozed.
Rocking the neighborhood had worn Figgy out.

"But Figgy," said George, "didn't you rest all day?"

The next afternoon, the Mustardos went to the Pizza Palace. "Figgy, we'll bring back meatza pizza for dinner!"

Figgy watched.

Figgy waited.

Figgy checked the clock.
It said WAY PAST DINNER.

Figgy could almost taste the pages in Mrs. Mustardo's *Bone Appétit* magazine, so he gobbled up all the recipes . . .

and fell asleep. Deeper and deeper he slept, and in his dreams, Figgy wasn't just a snorin', borin', nothin'-to-do dog anymore.

He was the one, the only

CHEF FIGGY MUTTSARELLO MUSTARDO!

Step right up for a piece of Italy's numero uno pizza! Try the delicioso Muttsarello! Or the FIGGY FIGARO!

Figgy woke up. *WOOF!* He knew his dream must be a sign. So he made his own: FREE PIZZA!

Every nose noticed and everyone nibbled.
Figgy Muttsarello! Figgy Muttsarello!
Figgy tossed and tossed—until he was too tired to taste!

WOOF!
"Figgy, we're home! Want your meatza pizza?"

Figgy curled 'round his tail and dozed.
All that pizza made Figgy a little sick and a lotta tired.

"What's wrong, boy?" George asked. "You're not even a little hungry?"

The next day, the Mustardos were off again. "Sorry, Figgy. No dogs allowed at the go-kart track!" said George. "We'll be home in a while."

Figgy watched.

Figgy waited.

Figgy checked the clock.
It said WAY PAST A WHILE.

When would they come back?
What else could he chew?
Figgy found something that
might have to do. He gobbled
George's race car box . . .

and fell asleep. Deeper and deeper
he slept, and in his dreams, Figgy
wasn't just a snoozin', losin',
nothin'-to-do dog anymore.

Figgy woke up. *WOOF!* He knew his dream must be a sign. So he made his own: FREE RACE!

Everyone raced! Everyone ran!

"Go, Speedy! Go, Speedy! GO! GO! GO!"

Figgy raced and ran until he ran out of race.

"Figgy, I'm back. Wanna fetch? Wanna run?"

Figgy was all raced out—too tired to wag, too tired to eat.

The Mustardos worried. Especially George.
"Figgy, what's wrong?"

When his family left *again* the next
day, Figgy sat by the window and waited.

Figgy had no one to play
with, nothing to do, and not
one thing left to eat.

He watched other families
play with their dogs, and other
dogs play with their friends.

Figgy was wide awake and all alone.
This had to be a sign. So Figgy made his own:

Everyone wanted a friend like Figgy, a rock-'n'-rollin', pizza-tossin', speedy-racin' kind of dog. But where were the Mustardos, especially George?

FREE DOG

WE LOVE YOU, FIGGY

Figgy searched the line from front
to back for any kind of sign.
Then he heard something.
"Yip-yip, Yap-yap!"
And then he heard someone.

"Figgy!" said George. "Here we are!"
But so was someone else.
Up popped a pup.
"Her name is Dot!"
The pup wobbled and wiggled and waggled.

Figgy wondered. Did George want Dot, not him?

Figgy ran.

Figgy dug.

Figgy hid.

"FIGGY, COME HOME! WANNA FETCH?
WANNA CHASE?"
But no one could find him.

Until Dot did.

"FIGGY!" cried George. "No more home alone for you. You've got me and now we've got Dot!"

Figgy sniffed Dot—she was only a pup, after all. She couldn't eat that much.

"WOOF, WOOF!" Figgy woofed.

This had to be a sign! So Figgy and Dot
made their own: FREE SHOW!
Everyone came. Everyone clapped.
Bravo, Figgy and Dot!

And from then on, Figgy had Dot.
And Dot had Figgy.

And the Mustardos, especially George,
had double dog trouble.